Gastown

Y.J.J.HAN

Here's a man standing on the street with short writings.
Sitting on the streets like snow, persons.

CONTENTS

dream

1.

We think of a ship that flies mainly
to the deeply space,
now there is a to be left in this humanity
where there is no one who
is flying along the boundaries of the universe.
We must lay the bridge in the night sky
that shines bright tonight.
We should not break the dream of
the young man who slept a stone pillow.
When this place is wide open,
it will send a pretty picture of ours
on their faraway ships,

2.

Today we must miss someone.
Waiting for the train to leave the empty station.
Maybe the old fog that
last night did not disappear.
To be able to recognize a dim shape in it,
I have to prepare for a story to share
with the flowing times sitting on

a bench commemorating someone with a friend,
who can know everything and know me first,

3.

Meet the ears of those who hide in the wall,
the whispers of those who are coming from
outside the window at dawn,
and the shadows that come behind the long
sundown, and tell us our stories.
It was the cries of the people who belonged to it
was. On unpaved roads,
anyone is left with a long footprint,
a trail to which point they should follow today,
a place where the stars disappear,
along the old walls of a place where they crumble.

painters

1.

Poor painters poured into the streets.
In cold weather,
they painted the city with hardened paint
and old brushes.
Silence began at the end of their hands,
and the city was reborn as a revolution of color.
Tamed doves by urban life will not leave here.
Where color cannot be discerned,
people will boast about the color of their lies.
Everyone is color blind.
Just like a nude that does not bother anything,
a painter who has lost a soul
and a deadly loophole make it color-blind
by drawing their own colors.

2.

Spring,
someday when we will all fade away
by the end of the season,
then it will be the only cold chill.
All the beasts of the prairies

will then leave here in search of a warm aura.
Where are we in the seasons
when we can no longer find the atmosphere
to be covered with dust,
the flock of goats to go to the highest places on
earth, and the flowers of our garden.

3.

If I see the world with the bird's eyes,
I will not be there,
because there is no place
to fold a shameful heart.
When we think of an old friend
who flew into the land of Eastern frozen Siberia,
there will be memories of us in their eyes,
the train is delayed,
and the beloved do not come.
If we sing to the world with a bird's mouth,
we will not be there to dance to the rhythm.

4.

A town isolated by heavy rains,
broken bridges, cats that lost their masters,
the nightfall of the sloping mountain streams,
the walkways have crumbled

and they have lost their way,
and this city has seen such a collapse,
The misinformation
and thorough alienation flow down the wet
buildings, the sorrows
and cries of those who have lost their masters,
the wet tents must be rolled,
the distinction of the land
where the stones of the unnamed people
and the stones of the old are built up,
Looking at the isolated temple,
seeing the collapse of the wandering people.

5.

sparrows and bustling,
the cuckoos and magpies,
and our hummingbirds
The names of the flowers
and the faces of the passing away
are buried untouched,
and their little songs revolves around us,
like ours that resemble
the waves of a small cobblestone
thrown on the lake memories
will call us from somewhere beyond,

change of season

The change of seasons resembles
the boundary of the mind.
During the turn of the seasons,
the universe will lose its guard
and drift away.
The glorious days of a distant empire
can no longer be expected of everlasting,
for those who have enjoyed
their rich days cannot be found.
Which border are we looking at now?
We will send hearts across
the Continent of Repentance to see
the migratory birds who have just learned
to fly away.

delusion of reed

1.

The reed forests rooted in dry land,
the sound of the bumps,
the deep stories of the nesting shorebirds.
Their roots will miss the mud drenched
in a deep breeze.
When the dry wind passes,
and someday they have to leave here,
the whispering swinging reed resembles their
crying. When the river rises there again,
Oh! That day was a day of their bright,
memories of prosperity,

2.

There is no reason to get out of delusion.
Waiting for the mist of this morning to be lifted,
I watch the parade going to the workplace
early in the daybreak.
Some of them will knock the frozen land
late at night and awaken the unconscious of
those who are sleeping quietly.
It is not strange for them to have no light.

Everything goes toward the end.
The sunshine is scarce,
and the delusions that float
in time climb over the heavily packed plaid streets
by sleeping one by one.

3.

Cracked ice walls,
breathing sounds that rise again every thousand
years, yet there are indelible shouts and footprints,
and where no one will disappear,
a small seed will be raised from a hiding place,
so this tough life and our trail will breathe.

standing on the boundary

1.

Those who have the boundary
between holiness and deceit,
and those who are too pure to measure their
distance. A premature infant who does not know
who their mother is takes a breath in the corner
of the street. For those who are on border,
and who will follow them into an endless abyss,
always have no idea which side to stand on

2.

The buried ones, and the long silence,
the fixed seasons that come back and forth,
the familiar faces that rise,
the names of the poor writers,
the birds on the banks of the river,
and the long funeral processions endlessly end.
I have never been brave before.
When I saw their shadows
that would be taken away,
I became a shadow trapped in the grey building
so that no one would hear it.

Someone shouted,
Our revolution was crazy,
we waved flags on the red building,
but the people who walked down the street
became plaster, as if they had never seen it,
and the snows that fell on the hard road covered
the clear bloodstains of the street.
I have never been brave there.
I have never been on the street.
I just stared silently through the misty window.

the land of resistance

1.

In the land of resistance,
the cat on the street is also scared.
The dream of rebellion will be growing
in their hearts that are quietly approaching.
Their language,
which has long been exploited and castrated,
has increasingly begun to acquire human speech.
The revolutionary army of the earth
that waited so long did not come,
and when the fears and tremors about
the trivial things spread like
an anesthetic shot into the whole body,
it began to show some sort of respect for those
which met in the street.
A situation tamed them.
The hidden instinct was covered with
a soft colored fabric.
Long boots were not visible,
but only the last fallen leaves of the season,
which had been crushed helplessly under the feet,
were wrapped around their ankles.
They might have envied the old settlers
who once walked on two feet

and contemplated them.
Now it is no longer necessary.
This is because the stone altar
that no one could touch and destroy are piled up.
On top of it,
the Milky Way of the Night sky comes down
and puts a ceremony.
Seriousness and piety are also tamed.

2.

I could not hate him.
Early dawned guests knocking on the door,
I knew I could not be forgotten.
The stones thrown at them will never make waves.
We must follow the sacrifice
of a young noble man.
We must shed a tear while looking at the back of
the one who carries holiness
and belonging together.
The praise of the blessed,
the comfort of the poor,
the pangs of the angry,
the rest of the weary,
and the breath of life.
Today,
the night scenery of one of the rural villages
is unusually brightened by the stellar stars

in the sky.

3.

The wanderers,
the barren sand hills
and the traces of a brief stay by us wandering
through the storm,
the hope for Oasis waited for the scattered cloud
to come together. It was not a short life.
There was always an old map of a world
that had been hidden beyond the horizon in its
pockets. When this hill changes again and
becomes a beach,
a small bottle of our walkway is washed away,
and we will stay with the welcoming
and forgotten of those who crave innocence
and build a castle together.
The sound of dust and wind scattered through
the air, and breaths and clear springs flowed.

missing

The little grasshopper's delicate sound
makes the autumn nightfall deeper into silence.
There is a blessing to think more,
and before this night is over,
we shall have some enlightenment.
The deep sound of the earth shaking millions of
years ago has not yet been woken up,
and all the precious things we have seen in space
are waiting for us in the deep earth.
When can we go there,
take out the faded paper,
and count the promises one by one?
Everywhere, anywhere was poor,
but tomorrow I will always think of
when I was thrilled with waiting.
The end of the wind from
there will never be cold,
so you will wake up from your deep sleep
and climb up the hill where the reeds shake.
The front side of discrimination is solitude,
the forest road without speculation goes into
a maze without exit, two walkers who forget
their names and walk silently,
and Deep underground is now trying to tell the
secret. Our wells have begun to dry from now on,

that we will not come again to water here again;
there we must hear the cries of wild birds
that their wings have broken.
The cry is like the voice of an orphan.
It resembles the story of a ginkgo
that did not grow up in front of the wasteland.
It was a farmer's cry over the ruins of a rural
village where one or two left.
I have to listen to the story of a child who was
born without knowing words affluence.
The land has never fallen,
but this place has become where stand up cannot
again, where we cannot go into orbit,
where can only live if we miss the past.

behind the moon

The old stories heard on Moai Island,
the lost language in the letters of
those who could not leave the land a long time
ago became stars in any universe.
The flock of eagles flying over the border
and the swarm of salmon that could not return to
the spawning grounds,
the children who could not remember them
and the town could not have everyone.
The frequent funeral procession
and the increasing cries of eagles were seen
in the mountain village where the cries of
newborn babies were no longer heard.
The only consolation was the firm conviction
that protected them.
I could not see the broken tracks
and the people trying to get to the peak.
I was looking for a footprint in the middle of the
desert, amidst the grief of the lost.
Where the image of the fossilized men was built,
there is nothing left behind their shadows,
Can we return to the back of the memory we
have been waiting for?
The Isle no longer spoke,
no more news in the wind,

in a desolate place,
where one has to miss.
We had to wait for it beyond the horizon
we were looking at,
an unfinished dry rainy season.
The waves did not rush to the beach,
just laying down the dead
and being washed down into the distant ocean,
our thoughts wandered beyond the horizon,
and we have to go where no one could expect
them. Standing on the back of the earth
at the sound of the waves,
hoping that someone would call
their forgotten name.

standing on the sundown hill,

I watch the wild flower beneath my feet,
lifting up its slender body to see everything in the
world. Have you heard their breaths
and their invincible vitality?
Even at night,
it will not bend over to get into its nest.
The air is no longer a narrow place.
The windage cannot shake its body,
so it will not fall anywhere.
It will not be silent in the rain
or wind anymore.
Nothing to be forgotten,
I wait for the souls of those who have crossed
the fence into the forbidden land.
Then we have to wait for the guests from another
land, so we will wake up the frozen lake
and realize that every moment we have to live
when it is warm again is not a burden.
When I realized that this was not a shabby place
that I could not live with,
there was no one left around.
I must miss something again.
I have no place to go on the ground
I have to listen to the faded leaves
and hear the sad story.

It is the time to close the doors on the ground.
Their shadows sleep between day and night.

the death of an actress

The sun does not set on the red sorghum field.
On the last way of an old actress,
we have to wait for someone.
In the passion of unknown actors
and nameless writers,
who will not yet come,
who will put down their soul,
the streets will not be frozen with their breath
and the heart of cold days.
Call out a name that is floating somewhere
on this street.
On a day when the city in wetlands were glorious,
we should wait to hear the applause of the
unknown audience, the heartless resignation song,
and the dance trapped in the shadows.
Every passing thing is meant to be,
but it is nothing to disappear with.
Those that break down in the waves of the beach,
those that will not return,
are the memories of the good old days,
and those who miss will go,
and where the wind stays on the hill,
will only leave traces of the sparrow.
By the time the parade of the long picnic is over,
now we must sit face to face with the end of

all the stories.
We must open the door for the soul that waits,
at any time our spring day will be.
Despair is also a sumptuosity;
looked at the river running on the broken bridge.
The fragment that breaks down on a wobbly
skeleton, she may be missing some glorious days
in such another world.

some wandering

No one waits on the mudflat.
I have long forgotten my time here.
I want to hear the story of a shell
without any feet that came up into
this space after wandering
thousands of kilometers under the sea.
This is not the place where I saw.
I see a reed with a broken stem in the field
that is holding his neck in peril.
It resembled a buried rebellion
and those unfinished revolutions
that had taken place in me.
The revolution turned the swamp into a cesspool.
I saw a rotted tree from the top of head.
The tree could not have gone through the winter.
Someday it will become a wilderness here too.
Even if I call a name,
there will be no twigs to answer the wind blowing
over its body. No pure man can be found on the
dust, and in the distant future,
himself who does not know
who he was will return here.
Who I was,
I will wait for the answer from the person
who decided to come.

Those people who knew me,
those myriad pieces that are falling down here,
when the puzzle aligned,
so imperceptibly, spring will come.
Ask me if I can get back the image
I lost in the beginning of time,
and when the season returns,
the density of the air in the east
and the dazzling sensation in the dawn fog,
I'll sing a song together
and say goodbye to me
that I've forgotten in that time,

may

I do not want to be parasitic again
in that season.
Friends!
That afternoon hundreds of rose flowers
fell in the square,
and I made a pledge not to boast of the glorious
days of youth again in this season.
They were not there,
and could not see the men
who had fallen down with the grass on the road,
nor the owl who had not been sleeping
in the middle of the night,
in the back of the village,
in keeping there.
So we had a sleepless night.
I saw the back of a camel falling down
with souls and thirst that I could not meet.
Cut the day off from the calendar
and place a candle on an altar
where no one can reach,
I saw the back of those who prostrated
with sorrow and dry branches
that could not make green leaves
despite the heavy rain of the season.
The birds of May who sat on the branches of the

tree and told us all about the day
were no longer there.
We cannot remember the face of mothers
who turned and cried before the dead
for a while now.
It was a series of days
that I could not remember again.
Youth has not been seen all day in a fog
that never disappears the shortcut to the deep
season, where there is no shade of trees anywhere,
is no longer parasitic.
If the fallen petals
are not in the shade of a tree
that they cannot rest comfortably,

wind

If you do not stand in the middle of it,
you will not know. You cannot hear their stories
unless you are at the center of an indifferent
density that comes from somewhere you cannot
touch and stays for a while.
There I see a soul of a miscarried woman
clutching famished.
Perhaps her story, which is not audible,
flows out of reach.
Screaming is heard in the dry forest.
The ancient glacier remained a mark on the rocks.
It was a gesture that hastened the last.
Knowing it beforehand,
the ungrown children on the hill were flying kites.
They were looking up a sunset hill with
the string of a kite that might break when.
Knowing everything, they were there.
So beautiful and strong,
they stood in the center
and talked to the old stories from afar.
Soul galaxies floating in space,
the depth of which was unknown.
I would like to find an ancient temple buried
in the sand of envoys
where I cannot still hear from them.

All I can hear is the sound of camels lost in the desert.

rainy season

The mother who lost the baby was crying,
wearing a long skirt made of hemp.
I have heard the story of a mountain village
that no one has ever been to.
I did not see the sun in the summer of that year.
Children were swept by the water in the valley has
risen due to the heavy rain
and reached to the village,
and there they hung on the branches,
and were waving in the wind,
with their swollen feet sticking out
as they were longing for sunlight.
The souls of the lost children were thundering.
The railing of the bridge,
which was broken by heavy rain,
was not seen at the end.
No one waited for the railroad to reach Seoul.
The lines of memory, lingering feelings of not
being able to connect to anything,
had to be discarded.
These marks will not be erased.
a day when the thick layers of curtains are lifted
to shine upon the traces of visitors on the ground,
when tears are stopped
and even wounds look beautiful;

I look at the flock of birds flying up the hill in
the east. They became crying there.
Sometimes, it is the only thing that scared so
many persons. They became us there and here.

old tree

You see the old trees of the often-visited forest,
the vines that grew up with the trunk of the tree
that our forefathers had seen together,
the strength of what they thought so deep and so
long, that the wind of the forest could not
overcome.
There is another cry to hear,
it was a longing for a new world
and a sign of areas to keep.
Whichever path you choose,
do not be tired on that way.
You will not feel hunger anymore
in this empty space
that you have come to this place,
you are my true friend and saint of deep thought.
We must send our sacred offerings to the desert,
so let us see the humility and the strong faith
that we have to fill the space
with our earnest wishes.
Never forget this place there
and send to the wanders on the dust your words
that wrote it down on the petals
that are lighter than the grass.
In this empty space,
which will be filled again even if it is empty,

I will always wait for a rich table.

serenade

This sorrow was not always tamed.
They had to listen to the drunken man's song
outside the broken window every night
because of the careless visitor's mockery and their
usual veiled conscience.
There were many nights of pain.
In the square, where our consciousness is buried,
in the dark, the requiem for some of us that
never end. I always had to watch the full moon of
April on the spot.
It was probably because of the song
that lasted until late at night
that I could not miss even in the old,
faded photo album.
On a day of thawing consciousness
and sensations,
on a long night that was short,
reminiscing over the colorful stage,
we should listen to a girl's tune.
Was she there?
Unshakable disillusionment
has often led to illusion.
The man, who was not the shy being,
kept his spot, constantly questioning the sound
and even giving himself up.

Now we have to wake up from our conscious
night. There is nowhere to go back,
but we need to stay awake
and have a new day with the souls who left.
The song to be sung for the day will be
circulating somewhere, and after this night,
I will listen again, my man! My songs!

arounding the border

If you look at water strider on the surface,
you have a vague idea of
how exciting it is to walk around the border.
When you look at the wonder of the unbreakable
things, the stubbornness under the moon light,
you look like the person you have wanted
to see so much.
When an unknown wind from the boundary
blows, an old face shuddered and buried
beneath the deep water rises.
I could not remember that day.
Everything was disappearing below the surface,
and the tremors that shook this place did not
know it was a little sobbing back then.
The time to wait until midnight has always been
fear. My obsession with everything
that was sinking made my legs
and arms stiff
and persons no longer looked for me.
There, I saw a girl becoming a plaster.
Strong buoyancy began to grow on the hard flesh.
The warriors who always live
with their dreams of immortality,
this empty gesture,
which seemed to catch the wind in a time

as fleeting as the Milky Way,
floating in the night sky,
where I cannot look back.

placard

The cries of the vagabonds
were heard on the garbage dumps,
which were not purged until the night of
disgust and nausea.
Their doodles and the mockery of
the unconscionable white classes,
anyone who takes away these turbulent products,
could have reached dawn.
In a country where flowers do not bloom,
when you call it by its name,
there are no living creatures here that can breathe.
Can you hear this cry,
a place full of cold cadavers under pressure?
When did you remember our beings?
Graffiti is another sanctuary,
where dream children grow up.
On the day these curtains are lifted up,
our revolution will begin,
and you will remember the names of those who
remain here that night.
Those who took the subway past midnight,
those wandering underground,
no one knew but me that they were warriors.
It was not the body that was shaking;
it was my spirit that was becoming impoverished.
On the day when the dream of revolution

disappeared,
there were only the advertisements of
the decadent tavern,
the prostitutes of the poor in the soul,
and the traces of the cats in the street.
All I hear is that you have to leave here
without hesitation,
but the rotten spirits that are tied up are
shaking and crying on the ground.

the eve of the revolution

1.

One night they left,
the last plane to the Europe in July
did not come back to where they landed.
The remnants are still far from spring,
but they can remember.
This place we live in is still waiting for
those who will return,
There will be another life there.
The red halo is still weeping
in that mountain range.
With our dirty hands still unwashing of
all the revolutions in the past,
we must take the next plane
that will not be delayed.
The things that are still available
to us are those that can bear
in the wide wing,

2.

Is it time for the sun to rise again on that wing?
Do we have to leave this place with
whom we are with you today?

The small birds that grow on the small
leaves are forgotten in their ears.
Red Square hid the rainwater flowing all night.
The clock tower in the square
will indicate the time
to go to the new site.
We remember that time.
Our little comrades!
Try to play the piano keys on untuned streets.
Let's meet on this wing when dawn comes.
Our lives will never be delayed.
Just as you cannot stop time,
you cannot stop the future of growing birds,

Song of a revolutionary

1.

Have you ever forgotten the night of March
that year when the moonlight always sat
on a dry branch over the window
and did not come down from there all night?
The sound of a cricket that forgot the seasons
knocked on the window all night
and the sound would call like my name,
and I would have lonely alone at dawn.
I saw the broken barrier around the yard.
I was afraid to cross the border every day,
so I did not open the window in the morning.
The wreckage of cold frosts gradually
penetrating into the underground,
the painful time makes it an unknown believer,
and the memories of last night's horror bring
pride and vain conviction.
The day will come when no one will come.
Then I will see the blackened space again,
and the fading fallen down by the ever smaller
sound. Have you ever forgotten the night with
the old flag and the little cry?
Absolute solitude that cannot wait for
anyone anymore!

2.

Where do you come from?
There is a place where the water does not dry
in the summer, unstoppable land, wildflowers are
full, and your footprint is clear in my sight.
Last spring, the hummingbird,
who stopped by for a while,
grows up all the time and spends plenty of honey.
The flowing time is also beautiful.
I will remember the young face of
my dispersed comrades.
When you leave a clear footprint to
where you came from,
the stars will follow the path.
Some poor and dreamy little girls will come with
me. Stars pouring out tonight call the wind.
Warm wind blows in my ear.
Loneliness does not fall in a spawning heart;
no one can stay in a space that cannot rest.
Their names fade away from their ears
and the boys who cannot grow up still stand
at the entrance to the village,
and his broken screams resemble
the sound of our songs that do not stop.

old man

Have you ever looked at the moonlight in this city?
Old man,
winds blowing through the pink buildings
they cannot stay this winter night.
The streetlight resembles the broken space ship
that dreamed of being a child from a Milky Way.
They have to dance and play
on the sidewalk block that will not stop.
Everyone is laughing.
Only the puppy who lost his master keeps
the last without leaving.
The dry thunder is not so amazing.
I hear the cries of those birds
that have not stepped on the dry land
in the underground river flowing through the city.
I remember the name of the knights
who left for the forest a long time ago.
Where they vanished,
I could touch the wind.
Cannot you see?
There to see the silver sunshine.

Friendly...

blue moon

1.

blue moon,
I went to school for my childhood,
which turned into ruins.
The fragments of shattered memory
are constantly making my past work.
Last time, the ginkgo trees of the campus
that have been preserved here do not grow up
as they did not grow up.
Where the friends of my childhood
who met me see where the pain is now,
the blue moon and stars that floats
above the mountains before the sun goes down,
the long time when they unfold like a floodlight,
the thoughts that have been entangled with
the flourishes that have grown up all the time.
This is always a hard workshop in my life.
When I turn on the light again
and replace the darkness,
I will be decorated with flowers
in this ruined place.
As my nostalgic friends,

2.

Where did the strength of the hidden shells
hiding and the strength of the mountains
that had changed over the countless years
and changed the lives of those who had been so
painful? When I realized the point of view
that there is no eternal longing,
I could only see the old piece of chalk hardened
into ruins and fallen in the pulpit.
The dry monsoon and lightning frustration
on the mountain ridge
that does not fall to the ground
sometimes shines on it. This city cannot
accommodate many crosses.
Every night we go up on the garden
and write down the obituary of those who went
up to heaven that night.
Do not forget this place.
I see a group of minnows living in a small puddle.
They know that.
A sad sound on a quiet land.
Their crying cries on the cross
that they cannot leave even when they leave.

3.

Shadows,

in the sinking the ever-lasting imagination
of the world, always tranquil we had to cross
the last train to the end of Europe at midnight.
There was no one on top of the summit,
breathless.
We waited for someone on the platform.
But it sounds like the sound of the dead men
heading home, in the shadow,
in despair with the imagination
that we can always meet this dawn for a long
night, we've been holding the railing of the
continents to the end.
The night cannot beat the dawn.
Dawn cannot overcome despair again.
We always repeat trips to the land every day.

the daffodils of april

1.

In one of the poor painters' chambers,
his splendid days, which he had never met before,
were being painted on the canvas.
The daffodils of april never faded.
He saw a time of young youth
who did not grow old or sad.
By the railroad track that is not always rusty,
the future children are gathering
and watching the stars in the night sky.
It would be a memory for the life that was in it.
The wind collects in one place and comforts
those who have to live with a passion.
People there! Flowers, our beautiful gardens!
Do not stay with the faded pictures in the drawers.
The fragments of nostalgia are attached to each
other. The precious moments that
he had with the memories of the painful days
came together in love with longing.

2.

Everything that stands on the hill has no fault,

no matter where I put it.
It will always resemble its humility.
The white snow-covered mountains
and the small seeds have now come to know
that there are so many of the deer
that resemble our traces, resembling us.
When I walked along the long riverbank,
there was always a railroad track to go to a place
where we wanted to go.
The zelkova in front of the town
where we rode with our younger companions
was still a big tree for us.
The old houses that lived together
were on the hill.
The song,
which the children sang along the stonewall
together, must be alive in our deep breath.
Now spring is coming soon.
A lovely time will come,
resembling the shy child,

clowns

In the fearsome heat that has come in decades
The weak have made the weaker
and the poor to fall into hell.
Someone told me.
As long as the fireballs deep in your heart
do not cool down
Fear will come from contention and death,
Ultimately,
divide the beautiful feelings of
all those living and breathing,
I will not let you go to the place
I have been searching for,
I will go quietly, threaten, and ridicule it,
Our clowns are gone,
that this land is no longer a stage,
He said he would teach me soon.
Hot heat will evaporate our innocence.
Behold the drift of those things
that have lost their emotions,
The spirit of spring,
The death of the berries
to be cooked red in summer.
I could not prepare anything at the time.
Brown harvest and
I lost the silent thought of the snow - covered
earth.

From the pilgrims who went to the east,
I could not receive a letter for that year.
These empty memories,
Souls of the earth who are in a starving spirit,

robin

Was it an early winter morning with frost?
I walked along the foggy forest path
to a small lake.
Already the surface of the lake
was covered with thin ice.
The frost was sitting on top of it.
The footprint of one of the little robins
was pinned tightly over it toward
the center of the lake.
My eyes face the middle of the lake along
the trail of three branches.
My feelings were also searching for
traces of a small bird in late fall,
which I grew up walking along a forest.
The mist in the forest has not faded away
and the air pressure accumulated early
in the morning wakes up all living things.
Last summer people raised a hue
and cry about the drying up of the land.
There was not the slightest regret
at the site of the fever.
They were not qualified to stroll
through this forest.
The traces of that little creature could not follow.
Pride and selfish spirits will soon fall asleep

under the weight of this fog,
and will become a treasure of the laughter
and verbosity of the salmon running back
a small valley each year.
I will always be small.
This lightness is fun.
I have to walk lightly to the center of the lake,
where it is hidden by dense fog
and I do not know what there is.

path, on any road

1.

Just as anything breaks easily according to clouds,
Falling down also follows established rules.
Spreading the alignment of time and space
In a crack that we have not seen in our home
It is preparing for the terrible time
for all the collapse.
As the course of the coming storm
and its weight cannot be measured
How should I meet
these suddenly inevitable times?
In the march of myriad pilgrims
As no one can predict
what steps will become true guides
When the light of the lighthouse is blurred
The dark seas have long voyages, losing the mark.
Someday, this little space where we stand
It will collapse according to clouds.
Where are you going to be trapped
in the sharpest and narrowest space?
Yet the end of the wind is not so cold
Before the waves are over,
before everything sinks
We must end this harsh and holy path.

2.

On any road

I confess that it is the most blessed way
to walk with someone who loves,
especially looking at the rising sun
through the thin clouds.
Today we sent to heaven a saint
who has a sincere heart like a shepherd
who was poor but lived honestly with anyone.
Thinking about those times
that were beautiful to anyone
We also know that when we leave things
that we have always held and leave
How pleasant it is.
I confess that he is a teacher
and lover of life.
Where is a gentle slope?
A person who is beautiful,
I always walk in the happiest memory,
thinking of only the flowering.
There is no quarrel.
A greed is like a steam that will easily disappear,
On this road or on any cobbled road
If you confess that, you are not sad,

mirage

I saw a mirage on the way back.
A stranger approaches, speaks,
and promises that I cannot keep.
I will contact you again.
I will write if necessary.
I did not enjoy friendliness.
Again, you experience the drift of language.
Someday this road will be over.
At that time,
you will not see a mirage from a distance.
One or two must leave this room.
I split the unit of time
and listen to the sound of bumping into
each other.
It is no stranger anymore.
Our neural networks come together like friends
and hang out.
I will contact you again.
No, I will not confirm.
Maybe even the friendliness
we have waited there will be a mirage.
Anyone can be welcomed.
A small change covers the city like a mist.
Even if the pressure fails
and the moments of joy collapse

I also wanted to make everyone happy.
It will look like a mirage
on the way back from far away.

I'm dreaming of a revolution.

One summer night,
beautiful sound flows
in the entrance of the village.
The moonlight is red,
and sometimes the cuckoo
in the forest does not sleep,
singing to the sound.
I followed the sound
and found a house with a small lamp lit.
In our small yard where we missed everybody,
There were some nice people
who seemed to meet sometime and danced.
The sound of the winds of the summer night
and the nostalgic family
And friends who did not grow up were beautiful.
I look for myself.
In the low place,
I sang a song with a drink of wine
that somebody would pour in my cup.
I was really blessed in my childhood.
If this time has not left my mood with
that moonlight,
The life of the garden!
If I sing together and drink the wine all night
and put embroidery on the night sky,

I will find the time of youth bound in love.
After waking up from a long sleep, if I knew that
it was a place of golden gorgeous youth

pieces of memory and a child

Pieces of memory
With the memories of the painful season
when we came back to our space
We will have to leave the strangers.
The space is struggling to support
a collapsed wall
that no one comes to.
In front of the rain that summer night
The dampness of the damp from the deep in the
earth, awakened by the sad cry of the scattered,
The leaves that survive the dying
and survive the harsh drought
do not lose their color,
If you gave me that life,
That this road like the desert was never lonely,
The pieces of memory that raised without notice
In front of their madness
We must always meet the late season.
We saw a water strider walking on
a polluted surface.
It is the place of their tryst,
We hear a blunt sound.
One night in a tranquil temple,
After the storm of the summer,
There we will meet a boy who collects sculptures.

We will meet innocent youth
who cross the desert without water.
We will not always be forgotten in the seasons,
This land will have glorious days
that we have never known,
The wind will go away,
and the sound of the flute of
the child will be heard,

my lamp

1.

Please remove that lamp
whose light inside is turned off.
No one will come to you tonight.
There are guests lying on the deep river floor.
I cannot hear the camel's crying,
and in the autumn night,
we will hear a cricket sound in the grass.
At that time,
I hope you do not think to avoid darkness
along the dark mountain road.
I just hope that the lamp will turn on again.
A messenger spoke.
The sound of the wind cannot be heard.
Still, the city's wetlands do not forsake hope.
Look at the feast of small flames on the wick.
Imagine the seasons of blooming on a small hill.
Please find my lamp's light.
Then the guys who lost their memories
on there will see the day
when their childhood dreams
will come alive again.

2.

There's no reason for the wall to fall.
It will probably do it because no one comes
or misses someone.
The struggle of the little birds
that have lost their nests will miss the wick of the
ramp. Whenever this void disappears,
it will be the day when some small light
among the dense stones will sound silently.
A small gathering on the side of the road
will be a pleasure of a rich dining table.
Then the little mountain will be greener,
the river will be deep and beautiful
and serene, my lamp!
Come back and light up the fire.

the man

1.

It was like an embarrassed excuse.
The castrated cats fell asleep on the shelf,
and the fallen cottages were
the only complaints of a long queue.
For what purpose do we have to keep this old city
that all of us have left tonight?
We remember that night that was gorgeous.
The days when the excuses of
those who lost a mate were
as beautiful as the cover of a childish magazine
that even tears.
We see the back of the man
who went into the deep mountain to build poetry.
The man who left countless excuses like
dust is probably our lost noble form.

2.

I see a picture in the background of a sea in the
wall. When the boundaries between the walls
and the sea were gone,
I saw an elderly man walking out of the picture.

He was no longer the weak.
Refusing the rank,
the boundary was pushed to the depths
of the coast by the waves.
I grew up to be a mature adult
and met people who stand with the wall
and shared a long story.
There is a moon in the night sky;
it always shines on the sea.
There are no boundaries,
so we cannot see the weak of the land anymore.

a forest way

1.

Memory makes another season
and a way that no one has walked in a forest
that has never walked.
Behold,
the calm words that permeates through the leaves,
the morning will come beautifully in every season
of our lives, and I will be the season for them.
There is a sound from small waterfall in the land
we wanted to see,
in our memories there is a school of our
childhood, a small hut,
and a school of cloisters dressed with ivy vines
that have few students.
Remember,
there is a place that is not forgotten
among the neighbors who call other seasons
and give warmth and greetings at any time.

2.

I see the history of old colonies at this grave.
I see a square tube and a colored corolla on it.

An old monument that nobody
cares about tells me to take off the chain.
You were the hero of history.
No, you were just a guest on a quiet earth.
All of us have lived differently
in the brittle history of colonialism,
and we only want to get out of this bridle
under the same sky last time together
with the wonderful corolla of the square.
There probably will not be a wind.
So you cannot see the flowers
that bloom in the spring.
The era of colonization will not be spring.
Is the night of colonization dark?
The wind is sleeping
and the full moon is a bright night.

commotion

There was a commotion in a small village.
Rioters that cannot be ignored never piled up
on the streets during the night of snow.
That night, no familiar drunken man could hear
the song again.
It was not that deep at night
and I could not find people.
Just inadvertently,
too much time is tied under dim mercury
lamppost, waiting for dawn to come.
At midnight,
buses that do not pick up passengers
are hit by falling snow from the night sky,
turning around the corner,
and only cats, who will live like the king of the
night, call their mates with unending cries.

the coastline

1.

The gray skies above the coastline,
the border, are pouring water
and then breathing. There is no gray fence.
The lost ocean current suffers from pneumonia
in the distant sea.
When the horizon crosses
the boundary like a fence,
we will have to wait for humpback whales,
taking a deep breath
and going on a trip to the deep sea
beyond this fence, seeing the sun sinking.
It was our face breathing
in the deep red sea,
resembling the old man's face.

2.

I see cutlass fish that have climbed from
the deep sea to the shore,
and I see fear in the eyes of villagers
living on the sea sinking down like darkness.
It was no longer the appearance of

those who survived the war in solidarity.
Deep under the sea, hollow shell washed up by
the sea and the waves began to control the
thoughts and words of the continental strangers
in the land to which the owner changed.
I had hoped long ago
that this sea could be a small hill
with easy-to-climb trees.
That was not my idea.
I would follow that long ago
when I could have gotten the idea of going
to the sea from an elk or roots
that got lost in the woods
and rotten raspberries from the roots.
The waves danced more violently.
From then on,
every time they saw an unknown creature
that climbed from the deep sea and died,
the villages of the territory began to disappear
one by one.

3.

I knew the blue sea,
the names on the sand dunes
that were not erased for a long time,
the wind blowing in the East.
At any given time,

I go to the place where my memories dancing,
where the stories of the mammals
that came from the land rising on the big water
hills are engraved. Waiting for the time
that the land will be connected
Waiting for the moon to light
the dark night sea to rise above that mountain.
I will miss the days of the red aged rather than
the blue youth,
and the sea will soon boil up.
Our days are brilliantly beautiful.

roadkill

1.

I watched a wild deer killed by a car
driving on Route 1.
The creature of the forest,
picking the last breath at the end of a long tire
trace, was the scene of a memory of dreams
that I had seen at some time.
I imagined the future of our land on the road
where the fog started,
holding a ritual in the forest
where I had lifted its body
as if it was asleep quietly.
Songs flow out among the tree branches.
The young birch lost its voices
throughout the winter,
and at the end of February,
it wanted to reap the wreck of the forest
and bring a warm aura.
Silence does not suit the season.
Old leaves falling down
against the branches of trees,
I am still treading the leaves for listening the weep,

2.

Who were we looking for
with the long procession of dead,
the images of funerals,
the sounds of a garden filled with moisture
and the cries of a bishop?
The only festival
that lost the joy of being overshadowed
by the spell of strangers
who were rescued from the village of silence.
No one wanted to go down the path of rough
gravel. The only ones whose purpose is
unknown were those who did not know.

3.

The mind is distracted
and the way to go this evening is far.
The darkness does not show the road already,
but the cuckoo that cannot find the nest is
ungainly and it is a common routine to homeless
on the road. In the light of the moon,
the clouds are flowing,
and finding the way ahead.
Have you ever felt such cold frost in the night?
Behind the hill leaping lightly,
my dear home will greet me.

pieces of revolution

1.

Puzzles of memorized pieces
in one night dream,
when waking up from a long sleep,
I penetrate into the unconscious again.
Looking at my familiar self
as I look out of the opaque window
as if I come back from a dreamlike walk.
This was a piece that was
well fitted to the shadows of people
who looked at the distant outskirts
of a strange neighborhood.
I am now jealous.
On a dead end street,
I see a different road.
A bright day will come.
The day will come when
I will shed tears to make you dazzle.
My pieces do not sleep until then.
The morning of the bright memory!
The dead are alive in that park.

2.

The refractions of the sound falling
on the branches,
the sob of those who have long
since left the earth.
The sighs of fishermen
who were polishing old fishing nets
and the wreckage
that crashed into the deep waters,
some crying was the sob of the dolphins trapped
in the aquarium.
This place is more like a sea
before it was created.
Today I see the brothers in their sweet days.

3.

Unknown poets all of the little insects
in the grass that did not wake up
to sleep were memories of a summer night.
In that month,
the full moon was covered in the clouds,
and only a deep breathing wind was heard.
It was a dark cloud that lasted for several days.
One day,
while waiting for these memories
to come back to their place,

the poet made a will for the world people
in a blank piece of paper
that would not be filled at night.

glaciers

1.

This is still the age of glaciers.
The frozen earth covered all our memories.
The end of the road
covered with snow was not seen,
and the ancient traces locked in a glacier
where the remainder of the horses
were lost were kept unchanged.
Where did their dreams begin?
Where the glacier melts
and where it comes from,
the crying ceases and the blizzard is still here,

2.

I am walking through the season of a thaw
that will someday be back,
the sea of memories I have missed and frozen.
I am looking at the fields of polar bears
and white wolves who lost their mother back
from land. Spores of seeds hid in deep grounds
without the appearance of a brilliant warrior
must have been rich meadows;

there were only sad stories of frozen emotions and aboriginal people returning to their vulgar world.

them or them

1.

This was a road
that had not yet been completed
and had never been.
How many of those huge cogs are waving here?
You see creatures that cannot sleep deeply,
other hidden Earth's mountains that cannot climb.
Pilgrims on the mountain path.
They are not coming back.
I could not despair.
Those who crave their names,
the shadows that resemble
the beasts of the mountains.
We cannot drift on the frozen sea.
Nothing more than the meaningless characters
in literature that crumble in it.

2.

The scattered characters
were put together again.
There is another lost civilization
in the place that could not leave.

Perhaps it would have been
their language to take off satellites
that would not be returned to a certain star
by densely packed cogs,
but we will not forget the words.
Poets and novelists
who left the land a long time ago
from which star are they writing letters
to the strange earth.
Their hearts were not cold.
In this frozen ground,

seasonal street

1.

The birds flying to the end of any mountain,
deep, did not come back.
They saw the railroad that followed
the two mountains.
The traces of coal that has been shed long
before the rusty railroad will not be lost here.
The day will run again.
Mahogany workers,
those who moved to the frozen ground,
did not return.
The mountain is always like that,
our long breath rusts,

2.

Where it started on the road
to a homely house,
nobody taught people who met on this way.
However,
the sincerity of the birds flying over
the fence could not bear the burden of
the stranger on the front door of any house.

The poverty separated us so that
the rich memories would now remain
as vain thoughts,
and the festival of thanksgiving
was held on the seasonal streets of the old
homeless. It will not be anywhere
in any part of the world,
but this desolate land was the dust
and the wind of the sand,
and the vain fog from the west.

old gardens

1.

Old gardens,
like the hands of somebody,
familiar stone sculptures,
and pictures of those children
who have not arrived yet,
figures in the walls spray-painted somewhere;
still our heart is snowy winter.
Today, we decided to meet folk at that time.
They are the promised traces.
The train to depart from midnight
will not be delayed anymore.
Even if the snow is piled up
and the children do not come,
it is always a garden that will not fall down.

2.

Its pieces of mind that are irreconcilable.
Strangers who forget their senses,
children who have lost their words,
babies who cannot grow up,
old people who can't go back to their nest,

have remembered a well in the middle of the
desert somewhere.
I came to an empty library today.
Where there was no one,
where there was no one to borrow books
or lend them, winter in the desert,
in the spirit of my ancestor,
there was an inexhaustible well.
It was the winter of life
when it was the last to cry.

3.

In the spring, the haze will bloom.
With the morning sun shining brightly,
along with those who climb up
the mountain with breathlessness,
in the minds of those who have to choose
on the two divided paths,
they must abandon the excitement of the new
day and the lingering fuss about
the beautiful northern winds
there will always be people waiting for us.
In these trivial times in this desolate village,

4.

Children's memories are locked,
the laughter of the young ladies seeping
around the stone walls,
the landscape that did not subside for joy
and their sighing sound
under the long winter night's horror light,
now we have to hide inside the morning haze.
Nothing has happened,
and you should keep rumors
about the day to those passing by.
The names of the comrades
and the long lengthening
that they left must be buried in a well
where the stars are sleeping
and the moon is dancing.

Gastown, the street of revolution

1.

Gastown,
city where the light does not fall,
on the red carpet,
some sleeping,
the streets where it does not freeze,
the flaming sun is rising over the sea
between a young John singing a flute
and a puppy,
Someday when the steam rising
on the surface of the water points to midnight,
there will be only the laughter
of the dancers and singers,
the Gentiles from faraway countries
and children who will come forward
with dreams of the future,
Oh, my spirit that will not forget!
The rubious sun that will rise from Deep Ocean!

2.

Horizon,
the place where we can see the boundaries,

which way to go there will not have to wander
again, Compass of companions
who lost friends and passengers under the moon,
we go on a long journey in caravan over midnight.
Somewhere,
even if they pass through a dry valley,
you will find a deep fountain
that somebody has uncovered,
and they will know that it is beautiful
and mild on there.

3.

When you look at the barren path
that anyone can take right of this unruly spirit,
and wait for this old garden to bloom,
you see the strange lovers
who broke up here one day,
and I remember that the wind's end was not so
cold, and the bugle of revolution is still ringing in
my ears, and the moon
that I see today is not the light of its shape
and in darkness,
Is the sound of those who tread
on the ground of the garden so intimate?

4.

The hot southerly wind continues to blow,
but trunk cannot go anywhere,
this is still a glacier island
where everything has frozen,
a long forgotten episode,
a small squirrel which has lost way through the
forest, a frost that has not melted overnight,
One tree covered with dry leaves
and a heart that avoids the cold;
That's how life is going!
What did you leave out
and how did you cry out in the world?
Young poet!
Your heart is always alive in the southern wind,

5.

When the most precious things were leaving
one by one, the Midnight Train,
which sought to calm the mind,
kept the spot without leaving the old platform.
At that time,
we scratched the rusty of all things
on the rusty rails
and we waited there at dawn every night.

6.

The unknown poems
and their cries,
the last dinner of the poor,
and the snowflake that ran hard that winter,
stood on the streets that season.
In the winter of thought,
the selfish criticism of the narrowed ones
and their binge eaters were ordered to them.
There will always be a seat at the edge of it.
Wherever you are, do not return.
A silent revolution did not end up
like a vulgar stone on the roadside.

7.

To live on the feet of the earth
means to endure the dirt,
dust and ooze blowing from the west;
our forests still do not sleep.
Could it be that the spring is not warm?
In a deceased world, early folly is tossed.
And when you leave a way alone,
things like the territory are dirty
and you just throw them away.
I see a small bird flying freely.

8.

I walked the streets paved with red bricks
I saw the faces that passed by,
I looked back with my eyes
and soul like the one I met at some time.
There I see only the back of many people,
and the face that I have seen is disappearing into
the back of everyone.
What planet has this fallen from?
What is this meteor shower?
I ride children's broken spaceship
and need to find my face again vanishing back
into a dream among the lonely crowd.

9.

I did not even know
that my shoes were dirty
and I was standing on the mud.
But I cannot take off my shoes.
I have to accept the remnants of filth
that come up to my heart as mine.
The lilies on the mud are beautiful all the time;
I cannot even make that flower,
if all things on earth were standing like that,

10.

There is a shadow
that waits so long.
Everything was right there.
Things that will disappear
leaving a long lasting day,
things that cannot catch anything it was a shadow.
It was a shadow to tempt me
to come around and hop.

{Books of Y.J.J.Han}

Novels:

Refugees, Ali
Hastings Street
Swine Fever

Collections of Poem:

The Old Memories of Tynehead
Space
Refugees
The Qs about Aiists
Epistles from the drifters
Wetland City
Gastown

NOTE

NOTE

NOTE

NOTE

NOTE

NOTE

NOTE

NOTE

NOTE

NOTE

www.ingramcontent.com/pod-product-compliance
Lightning Source LLC
Chambersburg PA
CBHW021931170626
46807CB00007B/3057